FERMÍN SO

ASTRO MOUSE
AND LIGHT BULB

PAPERCUTZ

NEW YORK

FERMÍN SOLÍS

ASTRO MOUSE
AND LIGHT BULB
#1 "Astro Mouse vs. Astro-Chicken"

FERMÍN SOLÍS
Script and Art

© Fermín Solís
© Bang. Ediciones, 2017-2021
contacto@bangediciones.com
All rights reserved.
Originally published as
Astro-Ratón y Bombillita #1: Parece que Chispea, 2008
and *Astro-Ratón y Bombillita #2: Pollo a la vista*, 2012
English translation and all other Editorial Material
© 2021 Papercutz
www.papercutz.com

Paperback ISBN: 978-1-5458-0638-8
Hardcover ISBN: 978-1-5458-0637-1

Special thanks to Stephanie Barrouillet, Agnés Phillippart,
Immaculada Bordell, Léa Jaillard, Maxi Luchini + Ed

Jeff Whitman – Translator, Letterer, Production, Editor
Ingrid Rios – Editorial Assistant
Jim Salicrup
Editor-in-Chief

Printed in China
April 2021

Papercutz books may be purchased for business or
promotional use. For information on bulk purchases
please contact Macmillan Corporate and Premium Sales
Department at (800) 221-7945 x5442.

Distributed by Macmillan
First Papercutz Printing

3

4

5

7

24

26

29

30

31

41

44

48

54

AH, YOU CAN ALMOST BREATHE IN THE PEACE AND CALM THAT'S IN DEEP, DEEP SPACE! THINGS DO LOOK A LITTLE BIT DIFFERENT AROUND HERE THOUGH... FUNNY!

64

69

70

"THE DINORHINOSAURUS ARE GINORMOUS CREATURES THAT WANDER THROUGH SPACE WAITING TO DEVOUR ANY AND ALL THINGS THAT DARE CROSS THEIR PATHS...

"I HAD THE BAD LUCK TO BUMP INTO ONE. IN THE BLINK OF AN EYE, IT POLISHED OFF MY SHIP AS AN APPETIZER AND THEN WENT ONTO THE WHOLE PLANET WHERE MY SHIP HAD LANDED.

"BUT WITH MY GREAT SKILL, I MANAGED TO ESCAPE THE SHIP, END UP IN THE BEAST'S NASAL CAVITY, AND PROVOKE A GREAT BIG MIGHTY SNEEEZE BY TICKLING IT A BIT... "

72

77

HERE WE ARE, PLANET GION!

THIS TIME YOU WON'T PLAY ME! LIGHT BULB IS COMING WITH ME AS A HOSTAGE, AND YOU, YOU WILL KEEP WATCH OF THE SHIP!

LET'S GO, LAMP, THE INHABITANTS OF PLANET GION NEED A HERO!

WE WILL NEVER SEE CACA AGAIN... AND POOR, POOR LIGHT BULB, IF I COULD ONLY DO SOMETHING, ANYTHING HERE...

PSSST!

EVERYTHING WENT BACK TO NORMAL
AFTER CACA WAS RESCUED...

HEY, CACA! YOU WANT TO PLAY?

HERE, GO FETCH IT!

WAIT A MINUTE, WHAT IS THIS?

YOU KNOW, LIGHT BULB, I DON'T KNOW IF WE DID THE RIGHT THING ABANDONING ASTRO-CHICKEN, EVEN IF HE WAS REALLY BOSSY...

ENTER THE COORDINATES OF PLANET GION. LET'S GO PLUCK A CHICKEN FROM THERE!

THIS IS CRAZY, ASTRO MOUSE! RETURNING HERE FOR ASTRO-CHICKEN...

HUH! WHAT IS THAT?

?

YOU MAY HAVE CAUGHT ME, BUT AS SOON AS I GET OUT OF THIS, YOU WILL SEE WHO'S THE BOSS...

SILENCE, BEAKY! TODAY WE ARE GOING TO FEAST ON CHICKEN WINGS!

AH, I GET IT. SO THE DISTRESS CALL WAS JUST A TRAP TO ATTRACT DINNER TO THE PLANET.

GULP!

106

WATCH OUT FOR PAPERCUTZ

Welcome to the funny, first ASTRO MOUSE AND LIGHT BULB graphic novel by Fermín Solís from Papercutz, that modern-day Rat Pack dedicated to publishing great graphic novels for all ages! I'm Jim Salicrup, the Earth-bound Editor-in-Chief and Space Force reject here to pontificate and possibly promote a plethora of Papercutz projects… Up until the publication of this ASTRO MOUSE AND LIGHT BULB graphic novel, it could be argued that Papercutz published so many graphic novels featuring felines we may as well change our name to Paper*catz*. Not only did we at one point publish GARFIELD, but we're currently publishing…

BRINA THE CAT—Brina's a big city cat that can't ever seem to stay at home. If she's not running wild in the countryside exploring the Great Outdoors she's outside of her family's apartment confronting a gang of angry rats on the City's mean streets. BRINA THE CAT author Giorgio Salati "tells an endearing tale…" according to *Publishers Weekly*, while *Kirkus Reviews* opines that artist Christian "Cornia's bright, expressive, animation-inspired art… is the main attraction of this series."

CHLOE & CARTOON—This spin-off series from the popular Charmz series CHLOE by writer Greg Tessier and artist Amandine, tells the tale of how a younger Chloe first met het pet cat Cartoon. The series features actual helpful information on the care and raising of a pet cat along with the same kind of fun stories that's made CHLOE such a hit.

CAT & CAT—The adventures of Catherine, better known to us as just "Cat," and her cat, Sushi, by writers Christophe Cazenove and Hervé Richez and artist Yrgane Ramon. In this series we get to witness the comic escapades of how Cat and her dad first adjusted to having Sushi join their family The fun continues as Cat's dad falls in love with a woman, who is a single mom with a son, and suddenly Cat and Sushi are now in a new blended family.

We could go on and on, mentioning such comical cats as Hubble — the unofficial mascot of THE GEEKY F@B 5, Azrael—Gargamel's pet and sole companion from THE SMURFS TALES, Hot Dog—Lola's pet cat (yes, Hot Dog is a cat!) from LOLA'S SUPER CLUB; Shahruk—Parvati's pet kitten/tiger from the super-hero series THE MYTHICS, and more, but we think you get the idea.

But never let it be said that Papercutz doesn't offer equal time to mice. While we're no longer publishing X-MICKEY (supernatural tales starring Mickey Mouse), MINNIE & DAISY, and THEA STILTON (which featured a group of five female mice who wanted to be reporters like their hero Thea Stilton), we are still publishing GERONIMO STILTON REPORTER (which not only features Geronimo, but his sister Thea Stilton too.), GERONIMO STILTON 3 IN 1 (collecting 3 original GERONIMO STILTON graphic novels in one new paperback edition), and now ASTRO MOUSE AND LIGHT BULB. The mice are *cat*ching up, you might say.

But when it comes to publishing graphic novels featuring sentient light bulbs and caca, we're outpacing all of our competitors! In fact, coming soon is ASTRO MOUSE AND LIGHT BULB #2 "Vs. The Troublesome 4," don't miss it! We hear a certain crooked chicken may be returning as well.

Thanks,

Jim

STAY IN TOUCH!

EMAIL: salicrup@papercutz.com
WEB: papercutz.com
TWITTER: @papercutzgn
INSTAGRAM: @papercutzgn
FACEBOOK: PAPERCUTZGRAPHICNOVELS
FAN MAIL: Papercutz, 160 Broadway,
Suite 700, East Wing
New York, NY 10038

GO TO PAPERCUTZ.COM AND SIGN UP FOR THE FREE PAPERCUTZ E-NEWSLETTER!

MORE GREAT GRAPHIC NOVEL SERIES AVAILABLE FROM PAPERCUTZ™

THE SMURFS TALES

THE ONLY LIVING GIRL

THE ONLY LIVING BOY

THE SISTERS

CAT & CAT

LOLA'S SUPER CLUB

ASTERIX

GERONIMO STILTON REPORTER

DINOSAUR EXPLORERS

GEEKY FAB 5

FUZZY BASEBALL

THE MYTHICS

THE RED SHOES

THE LITTLE MERMAID

BLUEBEARD

GILLBERT

THE LOUD HOUSE

MELOWY

ATTACK OF THE STUFF

GUMBY

PAPERCUTZ™
papercutz.com

Also available as ebooks wherever ebooks are sold.